A Gift for You

~~~~~~~~~~~~~~~~

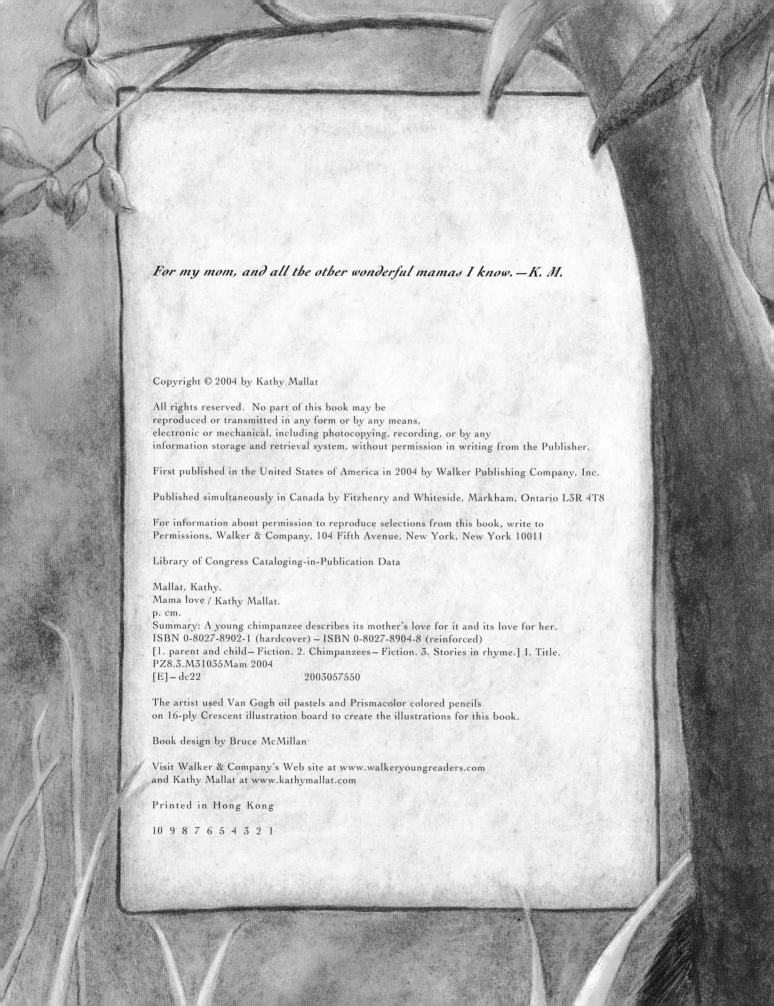

For my mom, and all the other wonderful mamas I know. —K. M.

First published in the United States of America in 2004 by Walker Publishing Company, Inc.

Published simultaneously in Canada by Fitzhenry and Whiteside, Markham, Ontario L3R 4T8

For information about permission to reproduce selections from this book, write to
Permissions, Walker & Company, 104 Fifth Avenue, New York, New York 10011

Library of Congress Cataloging-in-Publication Data

Mallat, Kathy.
Mama love / Kathy Mallat.
p. cm.
Summary: A young chimpanzee describes its mother's love for it and its love for her.
ISBN 0-8027-8902-1 (hardcover) – ISBN 0-8027-8904-8 (reinforced)
[1. parent and child– Fiction. 2. Chimpanzees– Fiction. 3. Stories in rhyme.] I. Title.
PZ8.3.M31035Mam 2004
[E]– dc22   2003057550

The artist used Van Gogh oil pastels and Prismacolor colored pencils
on 16-ply Crescent illustration board to create the illustrations for this book.

Book design by Bruce McMillan

Visit Walker & Company's Web site at www.walkeryoungreaders.com
and Kathy Mallat at www.kathymallat.com

Printed in Hong Kong

10 9 8 7 6 5 4 3 2 1

My mama loves me.
I'm the twinkle in her eye,
her heart's pitter-patter,
her star in the sky.

My mama loves me.
I'm her absolute delight.

She guides me and protects me through each day and night.

Mama shares . . .

and is quite inventive.

and brave . . .

and very attentive.

I love my mama.
She is everything to me,
the rays of my sunshine,
the roots of my tree.